ROCKET Out of the PARK

ROCKET Out of the PARK

Written by Andrea Cascardi

Dot. the TV series is based on the book *Dot.* written by Randi Zuckerberg.

First edition 2019

Library of Congress Catalog Card Number 2018961808
ISBN 978-1-5362-0009-6 (hardcover)
ISBN 978-1-5362-0312-7 (paperback)

19 20 21 22 23 24 LEO 10 9 8 7 6 5 4 3 2 1

Printed in Heshan, Guangdong, China

This book was typeset in Napoleone Slab.
The illustrations were created digitally.

Candlewick Entertainment
an imprint of
Candlewick Press
99 Dover Street
Somerville, Massachusetts 02144

visit us at www.candlewick.com

Contents

Chapter 1

FIZZ POWER

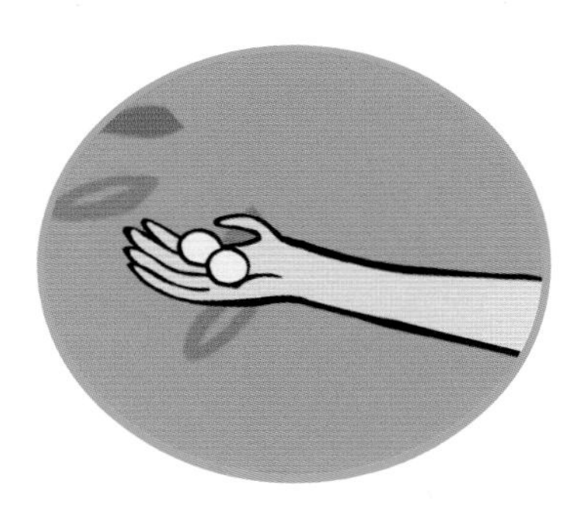

Dot and Mom went to the Creative Fair. There were awesome art projects and inventions everywhere!

"How will the judges choose the best thing?" Dot asked.

"There are no judges," said Mom. "This fair is about people making things and having fun."

Hal, Ruby, Nev, and Dev ran up to them.

"Is everyone ready for fun?" asked Mom. "I'm going to show you how to build fizz-powered rockets. We'll combine water and an antacid. That's the thing grown-ups take when they have an upset stomach."

Mom dropped an antacid tablet into a bottle of water. She lightly twisted the cap. The water fizzed.

“Those bubbles are full of gas. When they rise to the surface and pop, the gas escapes. It has to go somewhere, so . . .”

POP! The cap burst off.

“That was some burp,” said Ruby.

Mom handed out instructions. Everyone got construction paper and a water bottle, where the water and antacid "engine" would go.

"Here are some decorations," Mom said. "Make your rocket ships your own!"

Dot asked, "Which ones will make our rockets go the farthest and the fastest?"

"None. If your rocket is heavier, it will go lower and slower," Mom said.

"That's no good. The best rocket has to fly super far and super fast," said Dot.

"It doesn't have to. But if that's what you want, go for it," said Mom.

Hal found a slide whistle in the box. “Check it out,” he said.

“Nice! But your rocket might not go super far and super fast if it’s too heavy,” Dot said.

“I want the stuff. I plan on making a real bang with my rocket,” Hal said.

Chapter 2

FAR AND FAST

Dot wrapped construction paper around her bottle. She put fins on the sides and a cone on top, then held up her finished rocket.

"There! Nothing will stop my rocket from going all the way to the moon! *Maybe* even *Mars*," Dot said.

Dot did not add decorations.

"I want to keep my rocket light so it will soar," she said.

Dot went to see how her friends were doing. First, she checked on Ruby.

"Did you know the less stuff you put on your rocket, the farther it will go?" said Dot.

"Yup! But I want mine to be flashy," said Ruby.

"Sparkly!" said Dot.

"I know, right? But I think it could use more glitter," said Ruby.

"Where? The outside is covered," said Dot.

"I'll put glitter inside. When it flies, it will leave a sparkling trail," said Ruby.

Dot went over to Nev and Dev.

"Do you want help making your rocket zoom?" she asked.

"No, thanks. We're making a crazy rocket," said Nev.

"And a messy one!" said Dev.

"I've never heard of a crazy, messy rocket before," said Dot. "Where is it?"

Dev held up a big balloon.

"Your mom said we could make our rocket any way we want," said Nev.

"So we made a balloon rocket," said Dev.

"Cool! But where's the rocket part?" asked Dot.

Nev drew a rocket on a piece of paper and taped it to the balloon.

“Do you want our engine?” asked Nev. She handed the antacid tablet to Dot.

“That will make my rocket go super fast. Thanks!” said Dot.

Dot went back to Hal.

“How’s your rocket?” she asked.

“Almost done! I used as many noisy things as I could find,” said Hal.

“Wow! I can’t even see the rocket,” said Dot.

Chapter 3

LIFTOFF!

"Rocketeers, it's time for liftoff! Safety glasses on," said Mom.

"Can I go first?" Dot asked.

"Sure. Is your antacid tablet in there?"

"Yup! Both of them," Dot said.

Mom poured water into Dot's rocket. She lightly twisted the cap.

"Set it down on the launchpad. We'll stand back," said Mom.

"Way, way back," said Dot.

"Here comes the fun part," said Mom. "Three! Two! One! Liftoff!"

Dot's rocket shot high and fast into the trees and out of sight.

“It went even farther and faster than I thought it would! That was the best,” said Dot.

Ruby went next.

"Three! Two! One! Liftoff!"

Ruby's rocket whirled and twirled. It snowed down glitter.

"Your rocket was like fireworks!" said Dot.

Nev and Dev were up next with their balloon rocket.

"Three! Two . . ."

They let their balloon go. It made a funny noise. It sprayed a messy cloud of shaving cream behind it.

"That was great!" said Ruby.

Last up was Hal. “I present the Bellblaster!” he said.

“Three! Two! One! Liftoff!”

At first nothing happened.

Then there was a huge noise as Hal's rocket bounced off the table and landed on the ground.

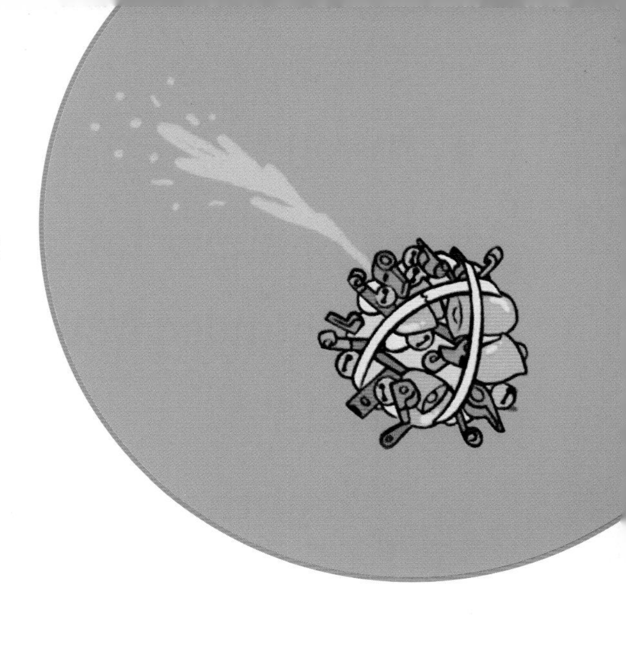

“Well,” said Dot, “your rocket didn’t go super far, but —”

“It sounded better than I hoped!” said Hal.

“All of the rockets were better than I imagined,” said Dot. “I guess a rocket doesn’t have to go super far or

super fast to be amazing. It can be super sparkly, super messy, or super loud!”

“Dot, where is your rocket?” asked Nev.

“I don’t know. It never came back down,” said Dot.

Chapter 4

ONE GIANT ROCKET

“I have one more,” said Mom. She wheeled in a giant rocket decorated with star stickers.

“You made that?” asked Dot.

“It’s huge!” said Hal.

The kids rushed to help Mom launch it.

Everyone stood way, way back.

“Three! Two! One! LIFTOFF!”

The giant rocket lifted off and flew high in the air.

Then it crashed to the ground.

Everyone cheered!

“At the fair, everyone’s rockets were TOTALLY different. And it turned out they were all great.

"And Dad found my rocket! I'll tell Hal so we can have another launch party. But this time, instead of using two engines, I'll use three.

"Maybe then it will go to the moon!"

"Time for me to unplug. This is Dot, signing off for now!"

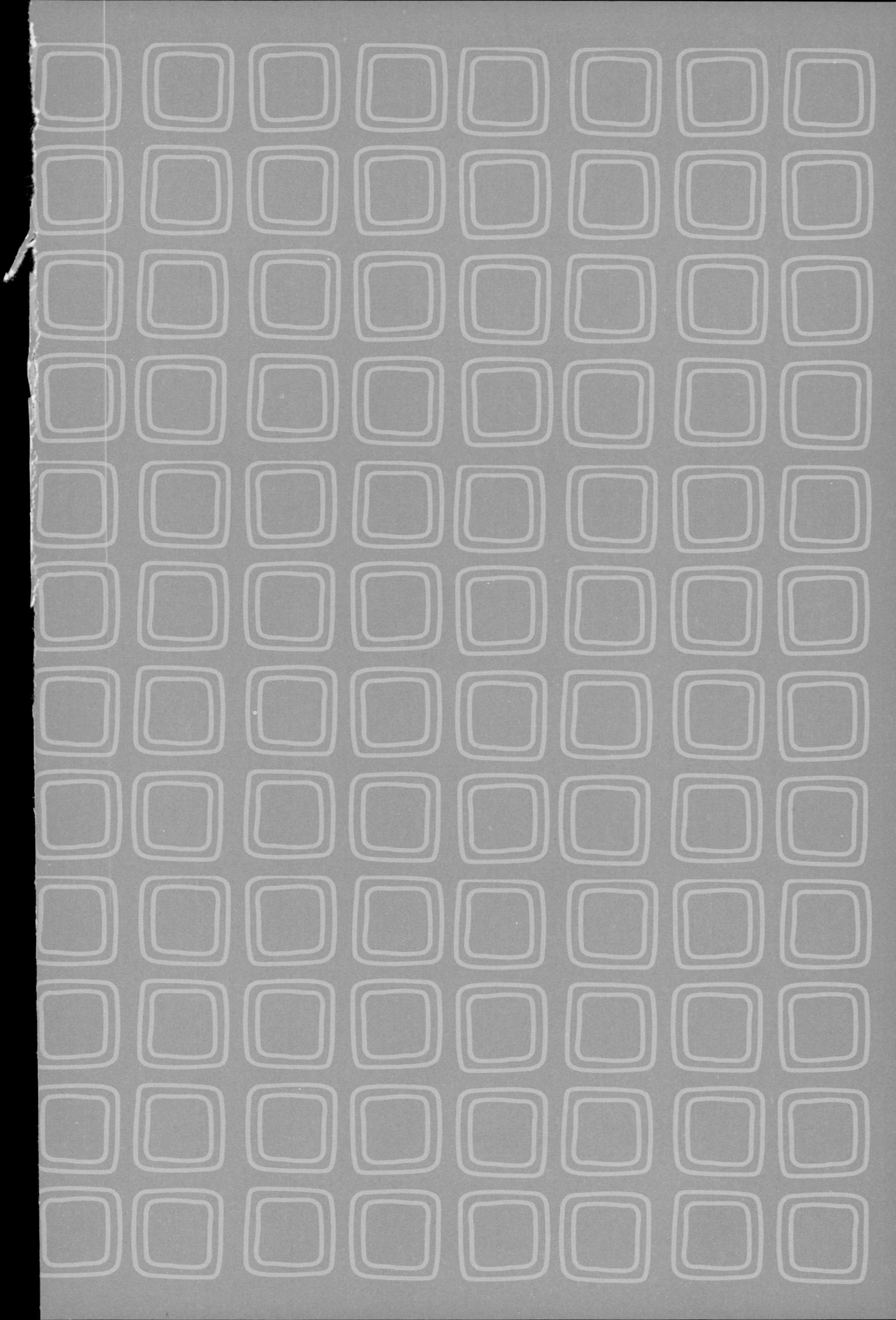

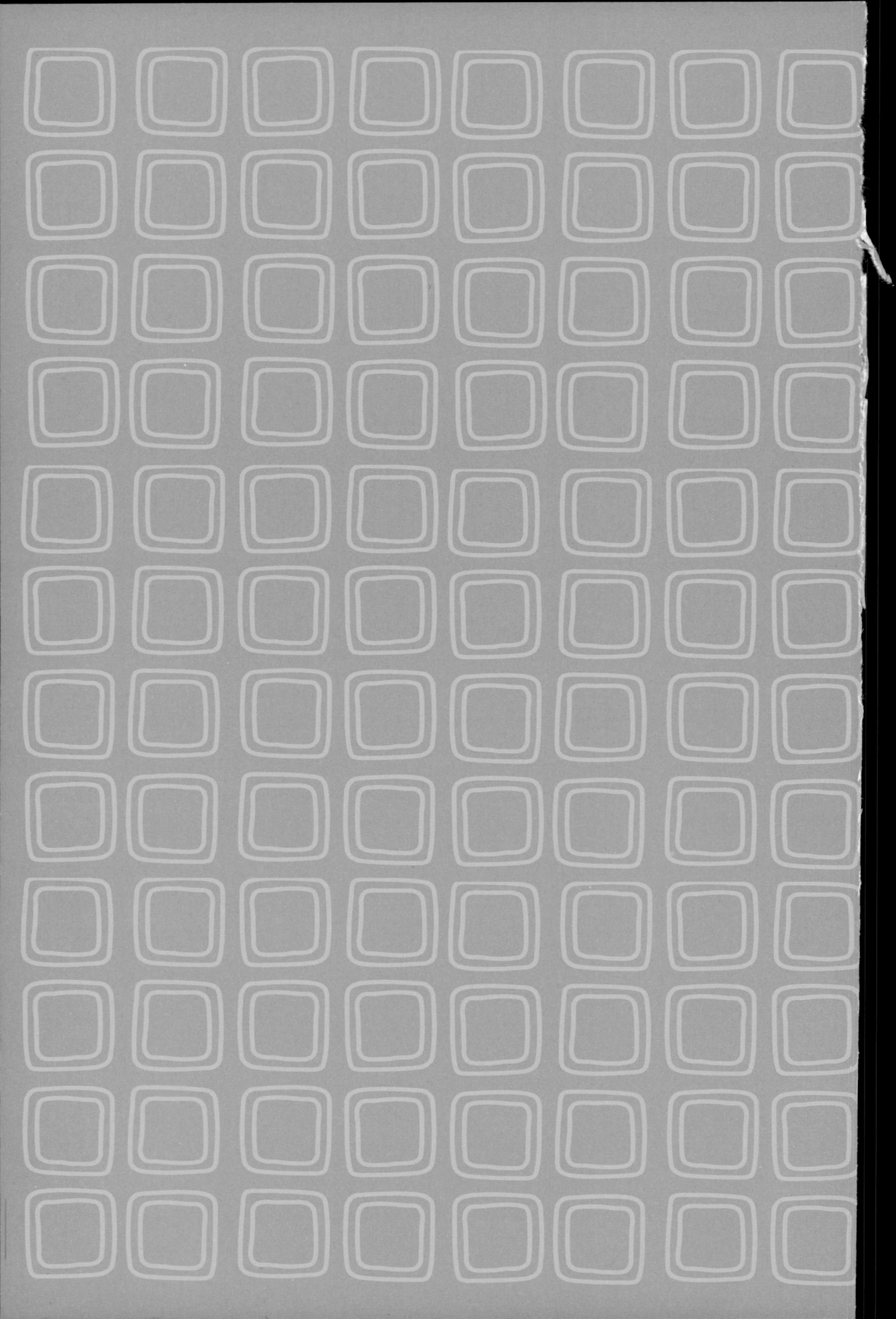